CHRISTMAS (penguin) CLASSICS

Give the gift of literature this Christmas.

Penguin Christmas Classics honor the power of literature to keep on giving through the ages. The five volumes in the series are not only our most beloved Christmas tales, they also have given us much of what we love about the holiday itself. *A Christmas Carol* revived in Victorian England such Christmas hallmarks as the Christmas tree, holiday cards, and caroling. The Yuletide yarns of Anthony Trollope popularized throughout the British Empire and around the world the trappings of Christmas in London. The holiday tales of Louisa May Alcott shaped the ideal of an American Christmas. *The Night Before Christmas* brought forth some of our earliest Christmas traditions as passed down through folktales. And *The Nutcracker* inspired the most famous ballet in history, one seen by millions in the twilight of every year.

Beautifully designed—with foil-stamped jackets, decorative endpapers, and nameplates for personalization—and printed in a small trim size that makes them perfect stocking stuffers, Penguin Christmas Classics embody the spirit of giving that is at the heart of our most time-honored stories about the holiday.

Collect all five Penguin Christmas Classics:

A Christmas Carol by Charles Dickens

Christmas at Thompson Hall: And Other Christmas Stories
by Anthony Trollope

A Merry Christmas: And Other Christmas Stories
by Louisa May Alcott

The Night Before Christmas by Nikolai Gogol

The Nutcracker by E. T. A. Hoffmann

THE NIGHT BEFORE CHRISTMAS

Written in 1831 by the father of Russian literature, this uproarious tale tells of the blacksmith Vakula's battle with the devil, who has stolen the moon and hidden it in his pocket, allowing him to wreak havoc on the village of Dikanka. Both the devil and Vakula are in love with Oksana, the most beautiful girl in Dikanka. Vakula is determined to win her over; the devil, equally determined, unleashes a snowstorm to thwart Vakula's efforts. Zany and mischievous, and drawing inspiration from the folktales of Gogol's far-flung village in Ukraine, *The Night Before Christmas* is the basis for many movie and opera adaptations, and is still read aloud to children on Christmas Eve in Ukraine and Russia.

PENGUIN ⊛ CLASSICS

THE NIGHT BEFORE CHRISTMAS

The son of a small landowner, **Nikolai Gogol** (1809–52) became famous for his short stories, among them "The Overcoat" and "Taras Bulba" and those in the two volumes of *Evenings on a Farm Near Dikanka*, a collection based on Ukrainian folklore. He held a chair in history at the University of St. Petersburg, and in 1836, when his controversial comic play *The Inspector General* was produced, he was hailed by critics as the head of the Naturalist school. The next twelve years he spent in voluntary exile, mainly in Rome. His panorama of Russian life, *Dead Souls*, was published in 1842 and was an immediate success. Gogol spent ten years working on a sequel; it was never to see publication.

Anna Summers is the editor and translator of two books by Ludmilla Petrushevskaya, *There Once Lived a Mother Who Loved Her Children, Until They Moved Back In: Three Novellas* and *There Once Lived a Girl Who Seduced Her Sister's Husband, and He Hanged Himself: Love Stories*, and the coeditor and cotranslator of Petrushevskaya's *There Once Lived a Woman Who Tried to Kill Her Neighbor's Baby: Scary Fairy Tales*. Born and raised in Moscow, she now lives in Cambridge, Massachusetts, where she is the literary editor of *The Baffler*.

Konstantin Makovsky (1839–1915) was one of the most celebrated artists in the Russian Empire in the nineteenth century.

Igor Grabar (1871–1960) was a student of Konstantin Makovsky's and a celebrated painter in his own right. He later became one of the premier art administrators in the Soviet Union, personally advising Joseph Stalin.

Aleksei Kivshenko (1851–95) was a Russian painter acclaimed for his depictions of historical subjects, especially battles.

The Night Before Christmas

Nikolai Gogol

Translated by
Anna Summers

·

Illustrations by
Konstantin Makovsky,
Igor Grabar, and Aleksei Kivshenko

PENGUIN BOOKS

PENGUIN BOOKS

Published by the Penguin Group
Penguin Group (USA) LLC
375 Hudson Street
New York, New York 10014

USA | Canada | UK | Ireland | Australia
New Zealand | India | South Africa | China
penguin.com
A Penguin Random House Company

This translation first published in Penguin Books 2014

Illustration credits
Page 22: Aleksei Kivshenko
Page 50: Igor Grabar
All other illustrations by Konstantin Makovsky

LIBRARY OF CONGRESS CATALOGING-IN-PUBLICATION DATA
Gogol', Nikolai Vasil'evich, 1809–1852, author.
[Noch' pered Rozhdestvom. English]
The night before Christmas / Nikolai Gogol ; translated by Anna Summers ;
illustrations by Konstantin Makovsky, Igor Grabar, and Aleksei Kivshenko.
pages : illustrations ; cm
ISBN 978-0-14-312248-7
I. Summers, Anna, translator.   II. Makovskii, Konstantin Egorovich, 1839–1915,
illustrator.   III. Grabar', Igor' Emmanuilovich, 1871–1960, illustrator.
IV. Kivshenko, Aleksei Daniilovich, 1851–1895, illustrator.   V. Title.
PG3333.N63 2014
891.73'3—dc23   2014012788

Printed in the United States of America
1   3   5   7   9   10   8   6   4   2

Set in LTC Cloister with Photoplay ITC
Designed by Sabrina Bowers

The Night Before Christmas

*T*HE DAY OF CHRISTMAS EVE ENDED, AND the night began, cold and clear. The stars and the crescent moon shone brightly upon the Christian world, helping all the good folks welcome the birth of our Savior. The cold grew sharper, yet the night was so quiet that one could hear the snow squeak under a traveler's boots from half a mile away. Caroling hadn't yet begun; village youths weren't yet crowded outside the windows waiting for treats; the moon alone peeked through, as though inviting the girls to finish up their toilette and run out onto the clean, sparkling snow. Just then one of the chimneys began to belch clouds of black smoke, and along with them, straddling a broom, flew out a witch. If Sorochintsy's property assessor happened to be passing

1

by on a troika of horses in his resplendent winter at-
tire, he surely would have noticed the witch, for that
remarkable man noticed everything: every piglet,
every bolt of cloth in a housewife's trunk, each house-
hold article her husband left at the tavern on Sunday.
But, unfortunately, the assessor wasn't anywhere in
the vicinity, and why would he be? He had his own
district to mind.

Unnoticed, the witch rose so high that one could
see only a little speck darting here and there, blotting
out the stars. The witch collected a whole sleeve full of
stars; there were only three or four left in the whole
sky. Suddenly another dot appeared in the distance
and quickly expanded, turning into something so odd
that even if you put on glasses the size of cart wheels
you wouldn't have believed what you were seeing.
From the front, the new creature looked like a regular German*: the narrow mug ended in a pig's snout
that constantly twitched and sniffed the air; the thin legs
seemed so brittle that if they belonged to the village

---

* By "German" we mean any foreigner, be it a French, Austro-
Hungarian, or Swedish subject—no matter, we will still call
them "Germans" (Gogol).

head of neighboring Yareski they'd snap the first time he danced a *kazachok*. From the back, the creature could be taken for a country attorney because of the long, thin tail that hung exactly like the tails on today's civil-service uniforms. Only the goatee, the small horns, and the creature's extreme griminess betrayed the truth: that this was no German or country attorney but just an ordinary devil who had one night left to roam among Christian folk and teach them devilish tricks. Tomorrow, at the first peal of church bells, he'd curl up his tail and scurry back to his lair.

The devil flew up to the moon, reached out and tried to grab it, but must have burned his fingers, for he hopped on one leg, sucking on his hand. He walked around it and tried again from the other side, and again jumped back. But the sly one didn't give up: he suddenly grabbed the moon with both hands and, juggling it like a hot pancake, stuffed it in his pocket, and flew off as though nothing had happened. In our village of Dikanka, no one noticed the theft. True, when the district scribe crawled out of the tavern on all fours he thought he saw the moon dancing in the sky, but who would believe him?

You'll ask me: why, for what wicked purpose did that evil creature perpetrate such an unconscionable act? I'll tell you. He knew that the deacon had invited Cossack Chub to a holiday dinner, which besides traditional *kutya* featured spiced vodka, saffron vodka, and other delectables. The guest list included Dikanka's village head; the deacon's kinsman, who owned a blue frock coat and sang the deepest notes in the bishop's choir; Cossack Sverbyguz; and many other prominent citizens. During that time Chub's beautiful daughter, Oksana, would have stayed home all by herself and would probably have received a visit from her admirer, blacksmith Vakula, who aggravated the devil even worse than Father Kondrat's sermons.

In his spare time, you see, the blacksmith dabbled in painting and actually enjoyed a considerable local reputation. The late Captain L. summoned him all the way to Poltava to paint his fence; every soup bowl in the village featured his brushwork. Even today you can find one of his icons in the church at the village of T. The pinnacle of his art was agreed to be a large panel inside the church porch, which depicted St. Peter expelling the devil from hell on the day of the

Last Judgment. Faced with imminent death, the terrified devil darts here and there, while the forgiven sinners bash him with whips and sticks. The devil tried everything to stop Vakula from finishing the hateful portrait, shoving his hand, blowing soot on the panel—but despite his heartiest efforts the painting was completed and nailed to the church wall, and since then the devil swore to take revenge on its creator. For only one more night could he roam freely and look for a way to pay Vakula back—hence the moon theft. He reasoned that Chub was lazy and hard to stir to action, and that the deacon lived not too close— all the way around the village, past the mill, past the cemetery, and around the ravine. On a moonlit night, maybe, spiced vodka could induce Chub to leave his warm bunk above the oven and undertake such a lengthy walk, but on a moonless night—unlikely. The wicked blacksmith didn't get along with Chub and, despite his enormous strength, wouldn't dare visit Oksana if her father were at home.

As soon as the moon disappeared into the devil's pocket, it became so utterly dark that no one could have found his way to the village tavern, let alone the deacon's house. The witch, finding herself surrounded by blackness, shrieked in fear, but the devil sidled up to her, took her gently by the arm, and whispered what men all over the world whisper to the fair sex. Can you believe it—the devil flirting? But that's life—everyone strives to imitate everyone else. Take our town, Mirgorod. It used to be that only the judge and the mayor owned fancy fur coats, while all the smaller fry wore plain sheepskin and didn't complain. These days, the assessor and junior magistrate both strut around in curly lamb covered with blue broadcloth; God knows how they afford it. Just three years ago I saw the lowly town clerk and district scribe shell out no less than six rubles a yard for some blue crepe de chine; the sexton, I've heard, commissioned wide nankeen *shalwar* pants and a striped worsted vest for the summer. What can I say? Every living creature wants to get on in the world, and the devil was no exception. The most grating aspect of his vile behavior was that he obviously fancied himself a sharp-looking fellow, whereas in truth it hurt one's eyes to look at him. But then the sky and everything below it grew so hopelessly dark that we couldn't tell you what happened between the handsome couple.

"So, *kum*,* you haven't seen the deacon's new place yet?" Chub addressed the tall, thin peasant in a short sheepskin, whose stubble hadn't been touched for at least two weeks by the piece of scythe that muzhiks use for a razor. "We'll have us a nice party there, I bet. I just don't want to be late." Chub tightened his belt, pulled down his hat, picked up his riding crop—the chief enemy of the idle village dogs—and was about to step off the porch when the sudden blackness stopped him in his tracks.

"What the . . . Look, Panas, the moon's gone."

"So it is," *kum* agreed phlegmatically.

"Right, and you just accept it, like that's the way it should be?"

---

* Parents and godparents of a child call each other *kum* (pronounced "koom"), or *kuma*, if she is a woman. The word indicates that they have become family through the ritual of baptism, without being related by blood.

7

"Well, what else can I do about it?"

"What devil has done this to the moon, I want to know? May he never have a shot of vodka in the morning," Chub cursed, wiping his moustache. "As if to mock us! I checked right before going out—a beautiful night, brighter than daylight. Now I put one foot out the door, and it's as if I've gone blind."

Chub grumbled for a while, considering the next step. He was dying to have a good chat with the deacon's other guests: Mikita the tar trader, for one, who traveled to Poltava every two weeks and brought back such jokes that all villagers split their sides from laughter. A full bottle of spiced vodka also caressed his imagination. The overall picture was very tempting, but the blackness of the night provoked his bottomless laziness, and he pictured even more vividly his warm cot and himself in it, smoking a pipe and listening through the doze to the carolers outside. If he had been alone he would have stayed, without a doubt, but *kum*'s presence made such an obvious display of laziness rather awkward. Chub finished cursing and addressed his *kum* again. "So no moon, eh?"

"None."

"Wonders. Can I have a pinch of your snuff? Such nice tobacco you always have; where do you buy it?"

"Nice? Wouldn't make an old chicken sneeze," *kum* complained, closing his bark snuffbox.

"I remember old innkeeper Zozulia once brought tobacco from Nezhin. What a tobacco it was! So, what shall we do, *kum*? Dark outside."

"Let's stay in," *kum* decided, and placed a hand on the door.

If *kum* hadn't said that, Chub would have certainly stayed, but now he just had to do the opposite. He took a decisive step off the porch. Immediately he regretted it but consoled himself that at least *he* had made the decision. *Kum* expressed no disappointment or surprise; he just sighed, scratched his back with a stick, and the two *kums* set off for the deacon's.

Now, let's see what Chub's beautiful daughter is up to.

Oksana wasn't yet seventeen. The whole world— that is, both sides of Dikanka—talked about her beauty. Young men followed her in hordes, and even if

9

she wore a potato sack she would have outshined all other girls. Oksana knew her reputation and behaved accordingly. Little by little her admirers lost patience and settled for less unattainable objects—all except Vakula, who continued his pursuit despite being treated as badly as the rest.

After her father left, Oksana sat for a long time at her little mirror, transfixed by her charming reflection. "Why did people decide to call me pretty? They just made it up; I'm not pretty at all." But the fresh face in the mirror with its shining black eyes and a charming smirk immediately proved the opposite. "Still, do they really think my eyes have no equals? And my lips? My nose? And what's so good about my raven braids? At night one might get scared by the way they wrap around my head like two serpents. No, I know I'm not beautiful at all." But the stunning reflection caught her eye again. "Of course I'm beautiful! How happy I'll make my husband! He'll forget himself, he'll choke me with kisses."

"Incredible," Vakula said to himself, entering the house quietly. "For a whole hour she's been staring at herself and still hasn't had enough."

"Is there anyone worthy of my beauty among those clowns?" Oksana continued. "Look how gracefully I walk, look at the ribbons in my hair, look at the rich gold braid my father bought me so I could marry the first among men!" At this she smirked again, turned around, and saw Vakula. The beauty frowned, blushing with annoyance, and the combination increased her loveliness to such a degree that no less than a million kisses could have done it justice.

"I see you got here fast enough. You all do, the moment father is out the door. Now, is my trunk ready?"

"It will be ready, my heart, as soon as the holidays are over. For two days I worked on it, didn't leave my smithy. The iron I used on it I didn't use even on the captain's carriage back in Poltava. And the decorations on it—you can walk everywhere and not find such beauty. Red and blue flowers all over it. Please don't scold me. Just let me look at you for a moment."

"Who forbids you to look?" Sitting down again on the bench, Oksana took up her mirror and examined anew her necklace, her braids, and her new blouse, and an expression of satisfied vanity lit up her features.

"May I sit next to you?" Vakula asked timidly.

"Go ahead," Oksana replied without changing expression.

"My wonderful, incomparable beauty, allow me to kiss you just once," the emboldened Vakula begged, pulling her toward him, but the moment the silky cheek seemed within his reach he was shoved away.

"What else would you like? Look at him: gets near the honey and demands a spoon to eat it with. Get away from me: your hands are hard like iron, and you reek of smoke. I think you got me all covered in soot." And again she took up her mirror.

"Oh, she doesn't love me," thought the wretched blacksmith. "She just toys with me, and I'm sitting here like a damn fool and can't take my eyes off her. Nothing I wouldn't give just to know her heart, whether she's in love with anyone. But she doesn't care, she just sits there, torturing me, while I see no sunshine for my wretchedness; no one will ever love her as much as I do."

"Is it true your mother's a witch?" Oksana asked him, and laughed so sweetly that the blood ran faster in Vakula's veins.

"What do I care for my mother? You are my father

and mother. If the Tsar summoned me tomorrow and said, 'Vakula, here's a smithy made of gold with silver hammers in it—take it,' I'd say, 'I want no gold or silver—just give me my Oksana.'"

"How sly you are! But my father is no fool, either. You'll see: he'll never marry your mother. But where is everyone? It's time to go caroling, and I'm getting bored."

"Are they so much fun?"

"More fun than you, that's for sure. Ah, I hear someone knocking, it must be them."

"She's just mocking me," thought poor Vakula. "She cares for me as little as for a rusted horseshoe. Well, at least I won't let anyone else mock me! Let's see who's winning her favor. I'll show him . . ."

A loud voice and the sound of knocking interrupted his thoughts.

"I'll get it," Vakula said, and ready to punch the first man who crossed the threshold, he went to open the door.

The frost was increasing. Up in the sky it had become so cold that the devil couldn't keep still and hopped from hoof to hoof, blowing on his numb fingers—understandable behavior in someone who spends his days in front of an enormous fire roasting sinners, just as our housewives roast sausages for Christmas.

The witch, too, felt the chill and, putting out her leg like a skater, descended through the cold air straight into her chimney as though down an icy hill. The devil followed her, and a moment later the two were crouching in her roomy oven among the pots.

The witch peeked outside to make sure her son, Vakula, hadn't brought guests. Seeing only coal sacks piled in the middle of the room, she climbed out, straightened her clothes, and a second later no one would have guessed that she had just enjoyed a ride on a broom.

Vakula's mother was no more than forty years old and was neither good nor bad looking (though, of course, it's difficult to look good at forty). Yet she so masterfully charmed gentlemen of a certain age that many local Cossacks paid her visits (admittedly, beauty wasn't first on their lists). And not one of them thought for a moment that he had rivals! A respectable citizen heading for church on Sunday or for the tavern in inclement weather often decided to stop by Solokha's, even if it meant a considerable detour. When Solokha attended a holiday service, clad in a blue frock coat over a colorful skirt with a silk apron, the deacon would cough and click his tongue, while the village head would smooth down his moustache, thinking, "Not bad, devil take me, not bad at all!"

Although Solokha was courteous with all the local Cossacks, a nosy observer would have noted that she was at her most cordial with old Chub. Chub was a widower. No less than eight stacks of wheat filled his front yard; two yokes of oxen mooed each time a cow or a bull walked past their stable; a goat bleated from the roof of his house like a traffic policeman, admonishing turkeys and chickens and showing his behind to the village boys. Chub's trunks were full of broadcloth and rich old garments—his late wife was into fashion. Besides the usual sunflower, poppy, and cabbage, his vegetable garden grew two rows of tobacco every year. All this Solokha planned to add to her own holdings, and she liked to imagine what shape Chub's property would take when it passed into her hands. To prevent it from falling into her son Vakula's possession, should he decide to marry Oksana, she resorted to the favorite strategy of all forty-year-old flirts: she pitted Vakula against Chub as often as she could.

Solokha's sly tricks inspired local gossip that she was a witch. A village youngster saw her tail, as big as a spindle; as recently as last Thursday she had run across someone's path in the shape of a black cat; according to the priest's wife, Solokha had walked into her house as a pig, crowed like a rooster, grabbed the priest's hat, and run off. The village shepherd reported he saw a witch walk into the manger, milk the cows, and then rub his lips with a substance so vile that he was spitting it for a week. All these reports were highly doubtful, for, as we know, only Sorochintsy's property assessor can spot a witch, which is why the respectable Cossacks ignored all the yakking.

Solokha began to tidy up her house without touching the coal sacks: Vakula brought them in, he could take them out. As for the devil, when he was about to go down the chimney he happened to glance back and notice Chub and *kum* already at a considerable distance from home. Instantly he flew over and began to dig up snowdrifts on both sides of the road, creating a blizzard. The air became white and thick with hurtling snow—any passerby risked getting his eyes, nose, and mouth clogged within seconds. The devil, pleased with his work, returned to the chimney. He was certain the blizzard would force Chub to turn back. On catching Vakula with his daughter, Chub was sure to give the blacksmith such a thrashing that for a long time he'd be unable to paint insulting caricatures.

*I*ndeed, as soon as the blizzard began, Chub bitterly regretted his decision and cursed himself, *kum*, and the devil. Chub's cursing, truth be told, wasn't altogether sincere. He welcomed the blizzard as a respectable excuse to turn back, which is what they promptly did. The wind now blew at their back, but they still couldn't see anything.

"Stop. We've lost the road," Chub yelled out to *kum*. "You go look for it over there, and I'll look over here." The road, however, was nowhere to be found. The only discovery *kum* made, plowing back and forth through the deep snow, was the tavern. It excited him so much that he forgot about Chub and the deacon's party and hurried inside, shaking off the snow.

In the meantime, Chub found the road and, soon afterward, his house. He yelled out to *kum* but got no response. The house was half buried in snow. Chub banged loudly on the door, summoning his daughter. But then he heard the blacksmith bark, "What do you want?"

Chub stepped back into the snow. "This can't be my house," he thought. "The blacksmith wouldn't dare come here. On the other hand, it's not his house, either. I know: it's lame Levchenko's, he recently took a young wife. His house looks like mine. But Levchenko is at the deacon's party, so why is the blacksmith here? Aha, I see: he visits Levchenko's wife!"

"Who are you, and what business have you here?" Vakula repeated more sternly, stepping closer to the indistinct shape.

"I'm not telling him who I am," thought Chub, "or the mean bastard will slug me."

"I'm just a poor caroler, dear host," he replied, changing his voice.

"Go to the devil with your carols. Go on now!"

Chub was of a mind to oblige, but he also felt annoyance at being ordered by the blacksmith and felt the need to talk back, as though the devil himself were provoking him.

"What are you yelling for? It's Christmas Eve. I came to sing carols, is all."

"Words aren't enough to send you off, eh?" And Chub received a painful jab on the shoulder.

"Jeez, you really lay it on," Chub grumbled, stepping back, and immediately received another blow on the back.

"Off with you," barked the blacksmith, and slammed the door shut.

"He thinks I won't find a way to rein him in? I'll go straight to the chief, he'll take care of that oaf, no matter he's a blacksmith and a painter. My back is probably all black and blue. Hmm. If he's here, that means he's not home; Solokha must be alone and lonesome. Hmm. Perhaps we could . . . a little. Hmm." The potential rewards awaiting him at Solokha's made the bruises and the cold seem less painful, and one could see through the snow that covered his face like shaving foam an anticipatory half smile.

During the devil's brief excursion out of and back to the chimney, his little side pouch got untied—and the moon slid out and rose slowly into the sky. The whole world changed. The blizzard died down, the ground lit up like a silvery desert, and even the cold seemed warmer. Bands of girls and boys carrying sacks with treats poured into the streets, and Christmas carols filled the air. What a gorgeous night! How can one describe the fun of mingling with the carolers? It's nice and warm under the sheepskin, the cold paints the young cheeks brighter, and the devil himself goads youngsters into mischief.

A group of laughing girls with full sacks ran into Oksana's house and surrounded the beauty, deafening Vakula with laughter and chatter. Everyone wanted to report what happened during their caroling and to show her their booty. Oksana seemed to enjoy herself thoroughly, to Vakula's annoyance, although he used

to be the liveliest caroler in the village. "Ah, Odarka," the beauty addressed one of her girlfriends, "you've got new shoes, and such lovely ones, with gold. You are lucky to have a man who can buy you shoes like that."

"Just say the word, my beauty," Vakula said at once. "I'll bring you shoes a noblewoman hasn't seen!"

"You? I doubt you can lay your hands on anything I would put on my feet. Maybe you'll get me what the empress wears, eh?"

The girls burst into laughter.

"That's right," the beauty announced proudly. "All of you, be my witness: if Vakula brings me the Tsarina's shoes, I give you my word I'll marry him right that moment." The girls led Oksana away, and Vakula followed them, his head hanging low. "Keep on laughing; am I not a laughingstock? I try to reason and can't—my mind is gone. Oksana doesn't love me—so what? Thank God the village is full of girls. She thinks only about clothes; she'll never make a good wife. No, it's time I dropped this nonsense." But some evil spirit kept pushing Oksana's image and her words about the Tsarina's shoes into his head; it was all he could think about. Groups of caroling girls and youths proceeded from house to house, but the blacksmith heard and saw nothing of the fun he had once enjoyed more than anyone.

*I*n the meantime, the devil had thoroughly relaxed at Solokha's. He covered her arm with kisses, clutched at his heart, sighed and moaned, and finally announced that unless she agreed to satisfy his passion, he'd go and drown himself, ruining his immortal soul. Solokha wasn't that cruel, and besides, they really were birds of a feather. She greatly enjoyed having a train of suitors, but this evening she expected to be alone, since every prominent villager was going to the deacon's. Only now this plan changed: no sooner had the devil declared his passion than they heard the voice of Dikanka's village head demanding to be let in. The hostess rushed to open the door, and the devil promptly jumped into the smallest of the coal sacks.

Having emptied a glass of vodka and shaken off the snow, the village head explained that he hadn't gone to the deacon's because of the sudden blizzard,

but then the light in Solokha's house gave him the idea that he might spend a pleasant evening in her company. Before he could finish, though, there was a loud knock, and they heard the deacon's voice. "Hide me somewhere, quick." The village head panicked. "I don't want him to see me." Solokha pondered hard where to conceal her corpulent admirer, then emptied the coal into the tub and stuffed the village head with all his outer garments into the largest sack.

Striding in, grunting and rubbing his hands, the deacon announced that no one had come to his party but that he was glad of the chance to have himself a little party with her and so had braved the blizzard. Then he sidled up to the hostess, coughed, smirked, and with his long fingers touched Solokha's full white arm.

"And what's this you have here, gorgeous Solokha?" he asked with a sly smile, taking a step back.

"Can't you see? It's an arm."

"Ha! An arm!" and, satisfied with such a beginning, the deacon strolled around the room.

"And how about this, dearest Solokha?" and he touched her lightly on the neck.

"Can't you see for yourself? It's a neck, and on the neck a necklace."

"Ha! A neck! A necklace!" and the deacon performed another victory lap.

"May I inquire, incomparable Solokha, what is . . ." the deacon began, and God knows what he would have touched if they hadn't heard Chub demanding to be admitted. The deacon went pale. "Oh dear, now Father Kondrat will find out, oh dear!" The deacon's fears, to be honest, mostly concerned his beloved spouse, who had already reduced his thick braid to a skinny ponytail. "For all that's dear, virtuous Solokha, hide me! Your kindness, as is written in Luke, chapter thir . . . Oh, anywhere, please!" Solokha promptly emptied another, smaller sack, and the not very large deacon fit there so nicely that you could easily pour quite a bit of coal on top.

"Well, hello, my dear," Chub announced, striding in. "Perhaps you didn't expect me? Perhaps you were entertaining someone else, eh?" His slow brain was clearly churning out a joke. "Perhaps you have company hidden somewhere, huh?" and, delighted with his wit, Chub let out a hoot of laughter. "Well, give us

a sip of vodka, that cursed cold has turned my hands to ice . . . What a night, what a blizzard . . ."

"Open up, Mother!" the blacksmith yelled, banging on the door.

"It's him, the cursed blacksmith! Solokha, you do what you want, but you must hide me from this bastard son of yours. May he grow bags under his eyes the size of a haystack!"

Solokha, who at this point lost her cool, darted around the room and in her terror gestured to Chub to get into the sack that already contained the deacon, who somehow managed not to groan when the heavy Cossack settled on top of him, shoving his iced boots into the deacon's ears.

Vakula stomped inside and fell on his cot without taking off his hat. One could see that he was in a terrible mood. Just as Solokha was closing the door behind him, there was yet another knock, and the last of the deacon's would-be guests, Cossack Sverbyguz, announced his desire to see her. Since he was taller than Chub's *kum* and heavier than Chub, there wasn't the slightest chance of hiding him, so Solokha stepped out into the yard in order to hear what he had to say.

The blacksmith was glancing distractedly around his house, listening to the singing of the carolers outside and finally registering the presence of two enormous coal sacks. "Through this stupid love of mine I've completely lost my senses," he thought. "Tomorrow's a holiday, and the house is full of rubbish. What are these coal sacks doing here? I should take them to the smithy," and he squatted down to tighten the knots. He was too distracted to hear either Chub hiss with pain when his hair got caught in the knot or the village head's hiccup.

"Am I not going to forget that worthless Oksana?" he continued his lament. "Lord knows I'm trying. She just fills my head against my will. But look at these sacks—they feel heavier than before. Perhaps there's something else in them besides coal. But I forget—everything these days seems heavier. I used to bend coins with my fingers, and now I quiver in the wind. But enough: I won't let anyone mock me!" And he cheerfully hoisted the sacks, which would have been too much for two strong men. "And this little one I'll grab, too—I believe I put my tools in there." He reached for the sack that contained the devil and marched outside whistling a merry tune.

The streets grew lively. Small windows opened one by one, and old mothers tossed pieces of sausage or pie to the carolers, who tried to catch the treats with their sacks. A group of boys surrounded several girls; elsewhere the girls surrounded one of the boys and made him trip in the snow. The magical night glittered with all its crystals, and the crescent moon shone all the more brightly on the white snow.

The blacksmith halted—he thought he heard Oksana's laughter. Every one of his nerves tingled; he dropped the two larger sacks in the snow—the deacon groaned, the village head hiccupped—and pushed his way into the young crowd. "There she is, standing like a tsarina surrounded by courtiers. That good-looking guy is telling her something amusing, and she is laughing at his joke . . ." Without knowing what he was doing, he squeezed through the circle surrounding Oksana and stood at her side.

"Ah, Vakula," she addressed him with the very smirk that made his knees buckle, "is this all you've earned with your carols?" and she pointed at the little sack containing the devil. "And what about my royal slippers? Don't forget, I'll marry you if you get them!" She laughed and ran off with her friends.

"No, I can't stand this any longer. Her eyes, her laugh—everything just burns me, burns me. I must put an end to this torture—farewell, my immortal soul; hello, the cold river." With a decisive step Vakula approached Oksana. "Good-bye, Oksana. Find yourself a fiancé you want, torture anyone you want, you won't see me again in this life." The beauty seemed taken aback and was about to say something, but Vakula just waved and walked off. "Where to, Vakula?" his friends shouted. "Farewell, friends. God willing, we'll see each other again in the next life. Tell Father Kondrat to pray for my sinful soul. Sorry I never had a chance to paint those candles! Give my things to the church. Farewell!"

"He's lost his mind," the young men said. "Oh, the ruined soul," an old woman passing by mumbled. "I must go tell everyone that the blacksmith has hanged himself!"

Vakula ran a couple blocks, then stopped to catch his breath. "What's the hurry?" he thought. "There's one last thing left to try: Round Patziuk. They say he's familiar with all the devils and can do anything he pleases. What's the difference? My soul's lost anyway." The delighted devil bounced up and down behind his back, but the blacksmith smoothed the sack with a hearty slap and strode off to Round Patziuk's.

This Patziuk had once belonged to the Zaporozhian Host, but whether he was expelled or left willingly no one knew. He had settled in Dikanka ten or fifteen years ago and at first lived like a true Zaporozhian: did nothing useful, slept three-quarters of the day, ate for six farmhands, and emptied a bucket of *horilka* at a time. There was room enough, it must be noted, for all that nourishment, for despite his short stature Patziuk was fantastically wide in girth. He also wore the widest *shalwar* in the village, so when he walked it was as though a wine barrel glided along the street. Days after his arrival it became known that Patziuk had a way with diseases and could cure anything just by whispering. Lately, though, he had stopped leaving the house, either because of his exceptional laziness or because he could no longer squeeze through his door. Those in need of his services had to come to him.

Not without trepidation, Vakula opened the door. A remarkable sight met his eyes. Patziuk was sitting on the floor in front of a small barrel with a bowl of noodles on top and, without touching it, was slurping the broth and swallowing the noodles. "Well, well," Vakula thought, "this one is even lazier than Chub—at least he eats with a spoon." Vakula cleared his throat. "I have heard, dear Patziuk—please don't take this in anger—that, well, you are rather familiar with the devil." Vakula paused here, half-expecting Patziuk to hurl the barrel with the noodles at his head and actually covering his face against the hot broth, but Patziuk only glanced at him and went back to his noodles. The emboldened blacksmith continued. "I came to you, Patziuk, may you prosper in every way and have enough of everything in proportion"— Vakula liked to use sophisticated words he'd picked up on his job in Poltava—"I came to you because nothing else helped me and you are my last resort. I'm in need, you see, of the devil's assistance. What should I do?"

"If you need the devil, you should go to the devil," responded Patziuk without raising his head from the bowl.

"That's why I came to seek your favor," and Vakula bowed again. "Except for you, no one seems to know the way."

Patziuk continued with his slurping.

"I beg you, dear neighbor, don't deny me this. Anything you need—pork, sausage, buckwheat, cloth, or anything else, as is customary among good neighbors—just tell me. Would you approximately describe the way?"

"If a man carries the devil on his shoulders, he doesn't have far to go," Patziuk said indifferently, without changing position. Vakula stared at him with his mouth open, as though ready to swallow the very first word of explanation like a noodle. But Patziuk said nothing else.

Suddenly Vakula noticed that the noodles and the barrel had disappeared and were replaced with two bowls, one with sour cream, the other with sweet dumplings. Despite his misery, Vakula was curious to see how lazy Patziuk would soak dumplings in sour cream and then eat them without using his hands. At that moment Patziuk opened his mouth and looked at the top dumpling sternly, then opened his mouth wider. The dumpling jumped from the bowl into the sour cream, flipped, and flew straight into Patziuk's mouth—all he had to do was chew and swallow. One dumpling tapped the stunned blacksmith on the lips, coating them in sour cream. Knocking it away and wiping his mouth, Vakula reflected on the many wonders in life and the lengths to which the devil can take you—though remembering that the very same devil was his last hope. "I should pay my respects again," he thought. "Maybe he'll agree to explain what he means . . . But what the hell's he doing? Tonight's Christmas Eve, and he's stuffing himself with cream . . . and here I am, tainting myself with sin!" And the devout blacksmith ran out of the house.

As soon as Vakula put down the sack, the devil, unable to contain his joy at capturing such a prize, jumped out of the sack and onto Vakula's shoulders.

Vakula's blood froze. He was about to make the sign of the cross, but the devil lowered his snout to Vakula's right ear and whispered sweetly, "Don't, I'm

your friend, your only friend. I'll help you out—
Oksana will be yours tonight."

The blacksmith pondered this. "Agreed," he said
finally. "For this price I'll be yours."

Delighted, the devil bounced up and down. I got
him, he thought, I got him. Now all the caricatures
will be paid for. He couldn't wait to see his colleagues'
reaction when they found out he had ensnared the
most devout Christian in the village. He giggled,
imagining how he'd tease his tailed coworkers, especially one lame devil who fancied himself the first of
tricksters.

He hurried to seal the deal. "As you've probably
heard, there's a little matter of a contract."

"Sure, I've heard. Blood, right? Here, I got a nail in
my back pocket," and Vakula reached behind and
grabbed the devil by the tail.

"Stop your jokes, silly," the devil giggled, but
Vakula made the sign of the cross, and the devil became as tame as a lamb. "Here," Vakula continued,
pulling the devil down and straddling him, "I'll teach
you how to tempt honest Christian folks." And he
raised a hand for another sign of the cross, but the

devil wailed pitifully, offering just about anything for his soul's precious freedom.

"This is how you sing now, cursed German. Get moving, go!"

"Where to?" the devil asked sadly.

"To St. Petersburg, to see the Tsarina. Go fast as a bird," Vakula ordered him, and almost swallowed his tongue when he felt himself rising in the air.

*F*or a long time Oksana stood pondering Vakula's last words. An inner voice told her that she had overdone it this time, that he might actually do something desperate—for example, stop calling her the first beauty of Dikanka. But no, she reassured herself, Vakula loved her too deeply, he wouldn't give her up. True, she'd been a touch too cruel—next time she'd allow him a little kiss. Satisfied with this decision, she skipped off merrily with her girlfriends.

Suddenly they stopped. "Just look at these monstrous sacks the blacksmith has dropped. Folks must have given him half a sheep for his caroling. We'll be feasting for weeks!"

"Let's take them to my house for a good look," Oksana suggested.

"Too heavy, we can't lift them."

"Let's fetch the sled!"

And the girls ran away.

By then the prisoners had grown pretty bored—even the deacon, who had poked himself a sizable hole. If it were not for the spectators, he would have come out; as it was, he only groaned under Chub's indelicate footwork. Chub, feeling that he was sitting on top of some supremely bumpy object, desired freedom no less. On hearing his daughter's directive, he decided to save himself a walk through the snow and wait for the ride home. Unfortunately, just when the girls left to fetch the sled, Chub's *kum* stepped out of the tavern in the worst of spirits: the proprietress had refused him credit, and as for the generous God-fearing villagers who might have treated him to a nightcap, they were all feasting at home with their families. Reflecting on Dikanka's moral decline and the proprietress's cruelty, *kum* stumbled upon the sacks. "My goodness, look at these monsters! I bet there's pork inside. Someone got lucky with his caroling. Even if it's just buckwheat pies it's a prize. Even if it's just plain loaves I'll be happy: the cursed woman will trade a shot of vodka for each loaf. But my God, aren't they heavy; I can't lift even one by myself."

Here Providence sent him the weaver Shapuvalenko.

"Hello there, Ostap! Which way are you going?" *kum* greeted him eagerly.

"Where my feet will carry me. Why?"

"Be a friend and help me carry one of these sacks. Some caroler has collected all this food and dropped it in the middle of the road. We'll divide it equally."

"These sacks? What do you think is in them, knishes or loaves?"

"Could be both."

They pulled out a couple of sticks from the nearest fence, hung one of the sacks on them, and hoisted the sticks on their shoulders.

"So where shall we take it—to the tavern?"

"I'd take it to the tavern, but the damn woman won't believe it's ours. She'll think we stole it. Besides,

I've just been there. No, let's take them to my house—wife's not home."

"You sure about that?"

"Hey, you think I'd offer if she was? I haven't lost my marbles. She'll be out with the hags till morning."

"Who's there?" thundered a voice from inside the house when the partners stumbled onto the porch. *Kum* and the weaver froze. *Kum*'s wife was the kind of treasure that's not at all rare in this world. Like her husband she was out all day, fawning over wealthy housewives who fed her; the spouses fought only in the morning, when they briefly intersected. Their house was twice as old as the district scribe's *shalwar*; parts of the roof were completely bald; the fence was practically nonexistent; the oven remained cold for days in a row. *Kum*'s gentle wife hid from her husband as well as she could everything she procured from the softhearted neighbors, and often took away his loot if he was too slow to pawn it at the tavern. Despite his phlegmatic nature, *kum* didn't cede his booty without a fight, and left the house almost daily with two black eyes, while his better half crawled on her rounds of the neighbors, groaning and rubbing her back, and complaining volubly about her husband's mistreatment.

Now you can appreciate the partners' shock. They dropped the sack and tried to block it, but too late: the old eyes were trained to see exactly such shapes.

"Aha. What is this?" the lady inquired with the excitement of a hungry vulture. "Good caroling, you two. Only I think it's not yours; you pinched it somewhere. Now. Let us take a look—right away."

"A devil might let you have a look, not us," *kum* responded, drawing himself up.

"That's right," the weaver piped up. "We caroled for this sack, not you. Stay away from it."

"You'll show me, you worthless drunkard," and the gentle wife punched her tall husband on the chin and made for the sack. The partners closed ranks and bravely repulsed the first attack, but before they had a chance to regroup, the enemy reappeared swinging an iron poker. She worked it deftly, hitting one on the back, the other on the knuckles, and before they knew it the partners were separated from their sack and shoved into the corner. "That poker of yours," complained the weaver, "what's it made of? My wife bought one last year—hers not so painful . . ."

The victor promptly untied the sack and was trying to identify the object inside. "Goodness, it's a whole pig," she concluded delightedly, eliciting a new torrent of grief from the corner. "Come, let's take it back," the weaver was encouraging *kum*. The partners stepped forward, full of fresh resolve, and the lady lifted her poker—but at that moment Chub stepped leisurely out of the sack, stretching as though after a good sleep.

"Goodness, and that stupid cow kept saying it was a pig," *kum* muttered. "How did he get into the sack—look at the size of him! Goodness take me— it's *kum*!" he exclaimed, recognizing Chub.

"Who did you think it was?" Chub chuckled. "But don't lose hope: there was something squirming around underneath me. Could be a pig or piglet."

The partners attacked the sack from one side, the lady from the other, and the battle would have resumed if the deacon, seeing that he had nowhere to hide, hadn't shown his burning face. The wife let go of the leg she was pulling; the weaver muttered something about the end of the world; Chub was stunned. "The deacon, in Solokha's sack! She must have had two men stashed in each sack all that time. And I thought she received only me . . . Devil take that woman!"

The girls were a little disappointed to find one of the sacks gone, but the other was still there, and they hoisted it on the sled and raced over the new snow. One or the other of the girls would jump on top of the village head, who had resolved to take the abuse stoically and only hiccupped. He was afraid the girls would think he was a devil, take fright, and run away, leaving him in the snow until the next morning. Finally, with laughter and giggles, the girls flung open the door to Oksana's house and dragged the sack inside. The hiccups that tormented the village head for an hour turned into a loud cough; the girls ran out the door screaming.

"Why on earth are you running like the house is on fire?" Chub asked them, walking in.

"Ah, father, there's a man in that sack!" Oksana cried out.

"And where did you find it?"

"On the road, where the blacksmith left it."

"So what are you screaming for? Let's take a look.

Sir, why don't you come out? Sorry for not addressing you by name."

The village head climbed out. The girls gasped. "Right," Chub thought, "of course, just like I said: a man in each sack. Solokha, Solokha . . ."

"Well," the village head addressed Chub after a pause. "How's the weather outside? Cold?"

"Chilly, but not too bad. Tell me, how do you polish your boots—with lard or with tar?" He meant to ask how the village head had found himself in the sack, but somehow his lips formed an entirely different question. "Tar's better," the village head replied, pulling on his hat. "Well, so long, Chub," and he strode out of the house. Chub stood gaping. "How come I asked him about the boots? But Solokha, what a devil of a woman! Look at her—a saint! Never touches meat on a holiday!"

But let us leave Chub to lament Solokha's betrayal and follow Vakula, because it's getting late—it must be after eight.

At first Vakula felt uneasy flying so high above the ground; passing under the crescent moon, he actually had to duck. But little by little he recovered and began to tease the devil, who sneezed and hiccupped every time Vakula touched his little cypress cross.

Everything glittered in the bright moonlight; the air was a transparent silvery mist. One could see everything that was happening in the sky: a wizard racing in his cauldron, stars playing hide-and-seek, a group of ghosts hanging together like a cloud, a devil dancing in the moonlight, a broomstick returning home after transporting a witch . . . All kinds of riffraff flew past them. Every creature slowed down to take a look at the blacksmith riding a devil, then continued on its way. Suddenly they saw a whole ocean of light—they had reached St. Petersburg. On approaching the city gate the devil turned into a magnificent mount, and Vakula rode horseback into the capital.

Oh dear, what noise, what light! Enormous four-story buildings lined the streets, trapping the noise from hooves and wheels; bridges shook under the carts and carriages; footmen and drivers screamed at each other; snow screeched under countless sleds; terrified pedestrians clung to the sidewalks, and their gigantic shadows danced on the walls, reaching the chimneys.

The stunned blacksmith stood gaping, feeling every building watch him with fiery eyes. He saw so many gentlemen in expensive fur coats that he didn't know when to tip his hat. "My God, how many gentlemen and ladies—look at all that fur and broadcloth; everyone who wears them must be at least a senator. And those who ride in those wondrous carriages with glass windows must be, if not mayors, then at least police chiefs." The devil interrupted Vakula's reflections: did Vakula intend to proceed directly to the Tsarina? "Lord help me, no . . . Somewhere in the city must be the delegation of Zaporozhian Cossacks who passed through Dikanka in the fall. I'd better ask them for counsel.

"Climb into my pocket and take me to the Zaporozhian delegation," Vakula ordered the devil. Instantly, the devil shrank and disappeared into Vakula's pocket; without knowing how, Vakula found himself in front of a large building and then in a gleaming room, where on the couches along the walls were sitting the Zaporozhian delegates, puffing on the strongest homegrown tobacco. Vakula bowed. "God bless you, gentlemen, what a joy to see you again!"

The delegates didn't recognize him at first. "It's me, Vakula the blacksmith from Dikanka, remember? You stayed with us for two days, may the Lord send you prosperity in everything. I changed the tire on your front wheel."

"Ah, it's that blacksmith who paints prettily. Well, brother, what brings you here?"

"Wanted to take a look. They say in St. Petersburg . . ."

"City big, eh?" the same Cossack interrupted Vakula, showing off his Russian, but Vakula held his ground. "City big, sure," he answered in the same language. "Huts all big, pictures, too, letters on signs all gold to the extreme. Wondrous proportion!"

The delegates were impressed with Vakula's fluency in the imperial language. "Well, we'll chat later; right now we must go see the Tsarina."

"The Tsarina? Be kind, dear sirs, and take me with you."

"You? To see the Tsarina? No, we can't. The Tsarina will be talking business with us," and the Cossack's face assumed an expression of mysterious importance.

"Do it," Vakula whispered to the devil, slapping his pocket.

"Let's take him, fellows, why not?"

"That's right, why not?"

"Come, put on a *zupan* like ours."

Vakula threw on a green Zaporozhian *zupan*, and a moment later a splendid footman announced that it was time to go. What a wonder it was to Vakula to ride in an enormous carriage on rubber tires with four-story buildings flying by. And the light! In Dikanka during the day they didn't have so much light. Finally the carriage stopped in front of the palace. The Cossacks stepped into a magnificent foyer and ascended an equally magnificent staircase.

"What a staircase! It feels wrong to step on it. What ornaments! I thought this was just in fairy tales, but no. Look at these banisters! They must have used fifty rubles' worth of iron on them." Following the delegates timidly, the blacksmith passed the first drawing room, then the second, then the third. In the fourth, Vakula walked up to the painting depicting Madonna and Child. "What wondrous skill. She could be talking, she could be alive, and the child is angelic, clutching his little hands, laughing. And the colors! I don't think they even touched ochre, only verdigris and mummy red. And the blue shines so—they must have used ceruse for foundation. But look at his brass doorknob: it is more artful than even the painting. What skill! Germans must have charged the top rate for it."

He would have continued his inspection, but the footman propelled him toward the other delegates. The Cossacks passed two more rooms and stopped—they were told to wait there. Several generals in gold epaulets strolled up and down, ignoring other supplicants. The delegates bowed four times, then waited. A moment later a tall, corpulent man in a hetman's uniform entered, followed by a large entourage; one of the man's eyes was half-closed, his dark hair disheveled. His whole manner showed he possessed the habit of governing. The generals surrounded him eagerly, following his every glance and gesture. But the hetman paid them no mind and walked up directly to the Cossacks, who bowed to the ground.

"Are you all here?" he asked them in a nasal voice.

"All here, father." They bowed again.

"You won't forget what I've taught you?"

"No, father, we won't."

"The Tsar?" the blacksmith asked the nearest Cossack.

"He's not just some tsar—he's Prince Potemkin."

There were voices, and the blacksmith was blinded by a multitude of glittering gowns and brocade coats. Immediately the Zaporozhians fell on the floor, wailed, "Have pity on us, *mamo*, have pity!" "Please get up," came a pleasant but authoritative voice. "Oh no, we won't, *mamo*. We'll die, but we won't get up!" The delegates continued to wail until the annoyed Potemkin whispered to their leader, and then the delegates got up on their feet and saw before them a short, plump woman with bright blue eyes and a smile that could belong only to a ruling monarch.

"The Prince has promised to acquaint me with my new subjects, whom I haven't yet met. Have you been well cared for?" the lady inquired with benign concern.

"Just fine, *mamo*; the grub here ain't as good as back home—but then you don't have our lamb." Potemkin wrinkled his nose at hearing the delegates say the opposite of what he had taught them.

The leader straightened his back and stepped

forward. "Have pity, *mamo*. What have we done to anger you? Have we shaken hands with the Tatars? Signed treaties with the Turks? Have we ever betrayed you in word or deed? Why such disfavor? First we hear you want to fortify against us; next, that you plan to turn us into a regular army. Now we hear of new misfortunes coming our way. What have we done to deserve them? Haven't we helped your generals cross the Perekop? Haven't we helped them beat the Crimeans?"

The empress seemed touched. "What do you want, then?" The Zaporozhians exchanged significant looks. "It's time," thought Vakula. He dropped to his knees. "Please, Your Royal Highness, what are your royal shoes made of? I can't imagine there's a cobbler in the whole country who could make shoes like these. If only my wife had a pair!"

The empress laughed at this, and so did her courtiers. Potemkin smiled and frowned simultaneously. The delegates, believing that the blacksmith had lost his mind, poked him furiously with their elbows.

"Rise," the empress addressed Vakula kindly. "If you want shoes like mine, that's easy to arrange. Right away there, bring him my most expensive pair, the ones with gold embroidery. Indeed, I find his simple manner appealing. Here's a worthy subject for your pen," she addressed a pale, modestly dressed man.

"Your Majesty is too kind." The man bowed. "This subject requires at least La Fontaine."

"No, no, I am still quite taken with your *Brigadier*. But tell me," she said, turning again to the delegates, "I've heard that Cossack warriors never marry."

"Sure we do, *mamo*, it won't do without a wife," answered the same Cossack, who for some reason used the roughest idiom with the empress—some clever politicking on his part, Vakula guessed. "We ain't some monks; we are plain sinners. There are many of us who have wives—some in Poland, some in the Ukraine, some as far as Turkey—only they don't camp out with us in the Sich."

In the meantime a pair of shoes was brought out for Vakula. "My God, look at these! If you skate in shoes like these, then what kind of feet must you have? Made of sugar, I imagine!"

The empress, who did in fact possess exceptionally lovely feet, couldn't help but smile at this compliment and at the blacksmith himself, who despite his olive skin looked quite dandy in his Zaporozhian dress. Encouraged by her benign attention, the blacksmith was about to interrogate the empress on everything he had always wanted to know—whether it was true, for example, that emperors eat only honey and bacon—but, feeling his neighbors' elbows, decided to stay quiet. When the older delegates began to inform the empress about their customs, he stepped back and whispered, "Get me out of here," and a moment later he was already beyond the city line.

"*He* drowned. I'll swear to it on anything," the weaver's wife declared to the congregation of Dikanka's housewives.

"What am I, a liar? Did I steal a cow from any of you? Or did I jinx anyone so now folks don't believe me?" shouted another female with a purple nose. "May I never drink water again if old Pepperchikha hadn't seen with her own eyes that the blacksmith hanged himself."

"Vakula? Hanged himself?" the village head wondered, stepping out of Chub's house. He stopped and joined the matrons to hear more.

"Water? You?" the weaver's wife screamed back at the purple nose. "You meant vodka, for sure. You have to be crazy to hang yourself. Drowned, I'm telling you; as surely as I know that you've just been at the pub."

"You worthless hussy, you shame me with the pub? And who receives the deacon every night?"

The weaver's wife turned scarlet. "Deacon? What deacon? What are you talking about?"

"Who said anything about my deacon?" the deacon's wife sang out, approaching the speakers. "I'll show you deacon!"

"This one here." The purple nose pointed at the weaver's wife.

"So it's you, slut, it's you, ugly witch, who casts spells on my deacon and feeds him poison to make him come back? May you never see your children again!" And the deacon's wife spat at her rival but instead hit the village head. "Ah, you dirty mongrel," yelped the village head, raising his whip. This caused the ladies to disperse with loud swearing. The village head continued to curse and wipe away the spit. "What filth! So the blacksmith drowned; my God, what a painter he was! And what scythes and plows he made—such

59

strength he had. Men like that are rare in Dikanka. Come to think of it, when he carried me in that sack I noticed the poor wretch seemed upset about something. And I was thinking of taking my piebald mare to him to be shod . . ." Full of these Christian thoughts, the village head walked slowly into his house.

Oksana felt disconcerted by the rumors of Vakula's suicide. She didn't hold much faith in Pepperchikha's eyes or the village women's gossip; also, she knew that devout Vakula would never put his salvation at risk by taking his own life. But to leave Dikanka for good— this was a possibility. Where else would she find another such admirer? And didn't he put up with her longer than the rest? The beauty tossed and turned in her bed all night—and by morning was up to her ears in love with Vakula.

Chub didn't express much emotion on learning about Vakula's fate. He was too preoccupied with Solokha's betrayal to think of anything else.

Christmas morning came. Before daybreak the church had filled with people. Older women in white kerchiefs gathered near the door; wealthier housewives in yellow and green cardigans congregated in the middle; girls sporting a whole shop's worth of ribbons and beads were trying to get near the icons; men filled the front—muzhiks with thick necks and thick moustaches, wealthier villagers in brown hooded cloaks over white and blue tunics. Everyone looked festive. The village head was smacking his lips, envisioning how he would break his fast on Christmas sausage; the girls, how they would go skating with the boys; the old women, mumbling their prayers with particular zest. The whole church echoed with the sound of Sverbyguz's forehead hitting the floor before the altar. Only Oksana stood sad and forlorn, thinking about Vakula, tears trembling on her eyelashes. Her girlfriends didn't suspect the reason for her misery. Others, too, were thinking about the blacksmith. The deacon had lost his voice during the ride in the sack and could barely squawk; the visiting bass did a fine job, but it would have been so much better if Vakula could have joined the choir in Lord's Prayer and Holy Cherubim, as he always did. Besides, he was the churchwarden. Matins were over, then the liturgy—but where was Vakula?

Vakula flew home even faster than before; in no time he was standing in front of his house, just as the roosters began to crow. The devil was about to run for it, but Vakula caught him by the tail: "Oh no, I haven't thanked you yet." And he smacked the devil three times with a switch before letting him go. Then he flopped in the hay and slept until lunch. Upon waking and seeing the afternoon sun, he realized he had slept right through matins and liturgy—a serious trespass on such a great holiday. The devout blacksmith decided that God had sent him that sinful sleep to punish him for contemplating suicide and vowed to go to confession that very week and to perform fifty bows daily all year. His house was empty—Solokha hadn't yet returned. With great care he unwrapped the royal shoes and again marveled at their craftsmanship. From the trunk he took out a new hat of curly lamb with a blue top and a magnificent embroidered sash, wrapped these gifts in a kerchief together with a crop, washed himself, put on his Zaporozhian dress, and went directly to Chub's.

Chub's eyes popped when he saw Vakula on his doorstep. He didn't know what amazed him more: the fact that Vakula had risen from the dead or that he had dared to show his face. He was even more amazed when the blacksmith opened the kerchief and knelt before Chub: "Here's a crop. Hit me with it as hard as your heart desires, only don't hold a grudge. Remember that you and my late father were friends, broke bread and drank vodka together."

It pleased Chub immensely to see the blacksmith kneeling at his feet—the blacksmith, who tipped his hat to no one in the whole village and bent coins like pancakes. He took the crop and slapped Vakula three times across the shoulders. "Here, remember to respect your elders. Now let's forget everything that's passed between us. Tell me what you want."

"Let me marry Oksana!"

Chub sighed, glanced at the superb hat and sash, remembered Solokha's betrayal, and said decisively, "So be it. Send the matchmakers."

Oksana walked into the room and gasped with joy and amazement.

"Look what shoes I brought you—the empress herself wore them."

"No, no, I don't need any shoes..." and she blushed deeply.

The blacksmith walked up to her, took her by the hand, and gently kissed her. The beauty lowered her blushing face—never had she looked lovelier.

*W*hen the late bishop, may he rest in peace, passed through Dikanka, he praised the beauty of its landscape and then stopped in front of a new house. A beautiful young woman holding a baby bowed to him from the porch. "Whose is this painting of a house?" the archbishop exclaimed.

"Vakula the blacksmith's," replied Oksana, for it was she.

"Fine work, very fine," the bishop said approvingly, examining Vakula's art. And there was plenty to examine: all the windows had scarlet borders, and on the doors Vakula had depicted Cossacks on horseback with pipes in their teeth. The bishop was even more impressed to learn that Vakula had fulfilled his vow and painted the entire left choir of the church with red flowers on a green background. But that wasn't all. Beside the church door he had drawn a portrait of the devil in hell, so unspeakably ugly that everyone spat at it as they walked in. If a mother wanted to distract a fussy baby, she'd bring it closer to the painting, saying, "Here, look, what a *yaka kaka*," and the fascinated child would hold back its tears, clutching at its mother's breast.